Ribbit!

Written by
Rodrigo Folgueira

Illustrated by
Poly Bernatene

This book is
dedicated to friendship,
especially ours.
—Rodrigo and Poly

Originally published in slightly different form in Great Britain by
Meadowside Children's Books, London, in 2012

No part of this publication may be reproduced, stored in a
retrieval system, or transmitted in any form or by any
means, electronic, mechanical, photocopying, recording,
or otherwise, without written permission of the publisher.
For information regarding permission, write to Alfred A. Knopf,
an imprint of Random House Children's Books, a division of
Penguin Random House LLC, 1745 Broadway, New York, NY 10019.

ISBN 978-1-338-18424-2

The publisher does not have any control over and does not assume
any responsibility for author or third-party websites or their content.

12 11 10 9 8 7 6 5 4 3 2 1   17 18 19 20 21 22

Printed in the U.S.A.   08

This edition first printing, January 2017

SCHOLASTIC INC.

Once upon a time, there was a pond that was home to a family of frogs.

It was their pond, and they were very happy living there.

But one morning,
they discovered
a surprise visitor. . . .

It was a pig—a little pink pig— sitting on a rock.

"**Goodness!**" said the frogs.
"Why is there a pig in our pond?"

They whispered amongst themselves,
until finally the chief frog spoke up:

"Ahem. Good morning.
What can we do for you?"

And, to their amazement,
the little pig answered . . .

"Ribbit!"

"WHAT did he say?"
cried the frogs.

"This pig is confused!"

"Does he think he's a frog?"

"Is he making fun of us?"

But again, all the little pig said was . . . .

"Ribbit!"

News of the little pig who thought he
was a frog spread fast, and all the animals
hurried to the pond to see the visitor. . . .

"This new relative of
yours is a little pink!"
said the raccoon.

"He's no relation of ours!"
declared the frogs.

"He certainly *sounds* like a frog . . . ,"
said the weasel.
"Why would a pig want to be a frog?"
said the parrot.

"And what's wrong
with being a frog,
may we ask?"
exclaimed the frogs.

Everyone started
shouting at each other,
completely ignoring the little pig . . .

The animals laughed and laughed—
and the frogs got angrier and angrier—
until, finally, the chief frog shouted out . . .

"Stop!

We're not getting anywhere by fighting!
We must go and find the wise old beetle.
He'll know what to do."

"The wise old beetle?"
gasped all the animals.

"But he hates to
be disturbed!"

"I know," said the chief frog.
"But this is very serious."

"That's true," the animals agreed.

And off they went.

And the little pig said . . .

"Ribbit?"

The animals found the wise
old beetle and tried to explain
the problem.

It was hard for him to understand,
because they were all talking
at once. In the end, he agreed
to go with them to the pond.

But when they arrived . . .

"Maybe," said the wise old beetle,
"he just wanted to make
new friends."

And off he went.

"Oh dear!" said the animals.

They hadn't thought of that!

"Tweet!"

And sure enough, sitting on
a branch, high up in a tree nearby,
was the little pig.

He was
surrounded by
new friends.